WIGGLESBOTTOM PRIMARY
THE MAGIC HAMSTER

PAMELA
BUTCHART

BECKA
MOOR

nosy
crow

WELCOME TO
WIGGLESBOTTOM PRIMARY!

MISS RILEY

HANA

JAYDEN

LAUREN

IRFAN

EVIE

MEGAN

MILES

SUSIE

MR HARRIS

SUNITA

ROZ

GAVIN

JOEL

ANNE MARIE

THEO

BOBBY

First published in 2016 by Nosy Crow Ltd
The Crow's Nest, 10a Lant Street
London SE1 1QR

www.nosycrow.com

ISBN: 978 0 85763 530 3

Nosy Crow and associated logos are trademarks and/or registered
trademarks of Nosy Crow Ltd

Text copyright © Pamela Butchart 2016
Cover and inside illustrations © Becka Moor, 2016

The right of Pamela Butchart and Becka Moor to be identified
as the author and illustrator respectively has been asserted.

All rights reserved

This book is sold subject to the condition that it shall not,
by way of trade or otherwise, be lent, hired out or circulated in any
form of binding or cover other than that in which it is published. No
part of this publication may be reproduced, stored in a retrieval
system, or transmitted in any form or by any means (electronic, mechanical,
photocopying, recording or otherwise) without the prior written permission
of Nosy Crow Ltd.

A CIP catalogue record for this book is available from the British Library.

Printed in Turkey by Imago.

Papers used by Nosy Crow are made from wood grown in
sustainable forests.

3 5 7 9 8 6 4 2

CONTENTS

THE MAGIC HAMSTER 3

FLY GIRL 33

ROBOT BOY 67

FOR COLE AND ORLA
P. B.

TO PAMELA
B. M.

THE MAGIC HAMSTER

Everyone went **WILD** when Miss Riley introduced us to the new class pet because we'd NEVER had a class pet before and also because it was a

HAMSTER.

EVERYONE

wanted to choose the hamster's name and Anne-Marie Moor wouldn't stop shouting

"PRINCESS HAIRY FACE! PRINCESS HAIRY FACE!"

over and over.

Miss Riley told us that everyone was allowed to put **ONE** name in the "Hamster Name Suggestion Box".

Everyone crossed their fingers and legs for luck when Miss Riley reached into the box and pulled out a name.

But when she read the name she looked a bit cross. And then she said, "Anne-Marie, how many suggestions did you put into the suggestion box?" But Anne-Marie wouldn't answer, and we knew it was because she'd probably put loads in.

So Miss Riley pulled out another name and it was **"RAVIOLI"**.

Miss Riley sighed and everyone cheered because we **LOVED** the name!

We learned all about hamsters and how
to take care of them **RESPONSIBLY**.
Miss Riley took Ravioli out of his cage and
showed us how to pick him up and hold him
without squeezing his little hamster bones.

Miss Riley said that every day a different person would be in charge of looking after Ravioli and that's when **EVERYONE** started screaming, "Me! Miss!

PLEASE! PICK ME! ME!"

But Miss Riley picked Megan McNally, and when Sunita Ram asked why, Miss Riley said that it was because Megan hadn't shouted like everyone else had and that part of taking care of Ravioli meant not frightening him.

All day, every time Ravioli squeaked, Megan jumped up **RIGHT AWAY** and gave him a sunflower seed. She even did it when she was in the middle of an argument with Sunita Ram about who broke the "Non-Shatter" ruler!

Then after lunch Megan started being **WEIRDLY NICE** to everyone. She let David Barry AND Bobby Henderson use her colouring pens even though she usually doesn't let **ANYONE** touch them, not even Miss Riley.

The next day, Theo Burke was in charge of Ravioli and he kept jumping up and giving Ravioli a sunflower seed every time he squeaked, just like Megan had. And then **HE** started being **WEIRDLY NICE** to everyone too! He even washed Sunita's paint pots even though she didn't ask him to.

That's when I noticed that Ravioli was giving people **THE EYE**. He would run up to the side of his cage when someone came near and then

FREEZE ON THE SPOT

and **STARE** at them with wide eyes for **AGES**.

Susie Keys must have noticed it too because she threw a scrunched-up piece of paper on to our desk which said:

DON'T LOOK INTO RAVIOLI'S EYES!

Susie Keys explained that Ravioli obviously wasn't a **NORMAL** hamster and that he was a

MAGIC HAMSTER

who could do hypnotism. That meant that Ravioli was controlling the minds of everyone who looked after him and that he was forcing them to do his **BIDDING** (which meant he was making them to do whatever he wanted, like bring him sunflower seeds every time he squeaked).

JUST as Susie said that, Ravioli squeaked and Theo Burke jumped up and gave him a sunflower seed.

"SEE?!" said Susie Keys. And that's when we knew that Susie was right.

Then all of a sudden Theo Burke said he felt sick and had to go to the nurse.

Susie Keys gasped and said that Ravioli's eyes probably go all swirly when he's hypnotising people and probably that had made Theo feel a bit sea-sick.

When we came back to class after lunch, Ravioli was sitting on Miss Riley's **KEYBOARD!**

We all knew that Ravioli must have hypnotised someone into letting him out of his cage but **NOBODY** would admit it.

The next day, Miss Riley put Sunita in charge of looking after Ravioli.

Miss Riley took Sunita over to Ravioli's cage and tried to show her how to take him out of his cage but Sunita kept her eyes shut **TIGHT** because she didn't want to get hypnotised. That's when Susie Keys said there might be a **CHANCE** that Ravioli **ATE PEOPLE**, and not just sunflower seeds, because he was staring at Sunita **SO MUCH** he looked like he wanted to eat her.

I was just about to say that I thought that was a SILLY idea because hamsters are tiny and there's no way they could eat a human girl but then Sunita

SCREAMED.

We all **RUSHED** over and saw that Sunita's finger was **BLEEDING!**

"Ravioli bit me!" she squealed and then she started crying. That's when **EVERYONE** shut their eyes and started screaming because we were all

TERRIFIED

of the magic hamster!

After Mr Harris had arrived and taken Ravioli away so everyone would stop screaming and open their eyes, Miss Riley explained that the only reason he had bitten Sunita was because she'd turned him upside-down and squeezed his head. And that she hadn't been paying proper attention when she picked him up.

Miss Riley said that Sunita must have given Ravioli a terrible fright and that he was **MUCH** more scared of us than we were of him and that we should be **GENTLE** with him and **NOT** scream near him.

Miss Riley also said that Ravioli **DEFINITELY** wasn't a human-eating hamster and that he was vegetarian, actually. And that made us all feel a lot better.

Once Sunita got a finger plaster, she asked Miss Riley why everyone who looked after Ravioli started acting weird and being really nice to everyone. And also why they did everything Ravioli told them to do, like feeding him seeds as **SOON** as he squeaked and letting him out of his cage.

And that's when Miss Jones explained that she'd told each helper to make sure to feed Ravioli if he squeaked, because he was still young and that meant he got hungry a lot.

Then Miss Riley said that she'd told every helper that if they were **SUPERGOOD** one of them would get to take Ravioli home **ALL WEEKEND**.

She also said that Theo must have left the cage open, by accident, when he wasn't feeling well and that that was how Ravioli had escaped.

So that's when we all realised that Ravioli **WASN'T** a hypnotising, human-eating hamster and we all felt bad about scaring him.

Sunita put up her hand and asked Miss Riley if she could

PLEASE

be the one to take him home for the weekend and that she would never **EVER** squeeze his head **OR** turn him upside down again, even if he bit her **FIVE HUNDRED** times. And Miss Riley smiled and said OK.

EVERYONE told Sunita how lucky she was and Sunita said that she completely

LOVED

Ravioli now and that he was her favourite **EVERYTHING**.

We all sat quictly with our fingers on our lips while Miss Riley brought Ravioli back into the classroom. And then we all took turns at petting him gently and saying sorry for scaring him.

We all giggled as we watched Ravioli fuss around while he made himself a big fluffy bed out of the cotton wool.

Then Theo came back to class and told us that the reason he'd felt sick was because Miss Riley had told him he'd have to clear the poo out of Ravioli's cage at the end of the day.

And then Sunita got a really weird look on her face and we all started giggling because we knew it was because she'd just realised that **SHE** would have to pick up Ravioli's poo **ALL WEEKEND**.

One day, Evie McIntosh swallowed a fly by mistake. It wasn't even a tiny fly, like the ones that like fruit. It was

HUGE.

EVERYONE was talking about it, even the Year 6s. **THAT'S** how big the fly had been.

Lauren Carr's big sister Hannah Carr even came over and whispered to us that if you swallow a fly you turn into one. But we didn't tell Evie that because we didn't want to worry her.

At first we all thought Evie was going to be sick because her face went a really weird colour and she said, "I'm going to be sick." But then she wasn't.

Theo Burke gave Evie **ALL** of his packed lunch, even though it was only morning break, and told her to eat it right away to get rid of the **FLY TASTE**.

So Evie ate Theo's packed lunch. And then she ate Anne-Marie Moor's chocolate biscuit (even though Anne-Marie hadn't said that she could).

After break when we were baking jam sponges in the activity room, Evie kept running everywhere and she had flour all over her hair, and jam on her glasses and she kept tasting **EVERYTHING** even though we weren't supposed to.

HOW TO BAKE
A CAKE

39

And when it was time to put our cakes in the oven and clear up, Evie sat by the oven and kept flicking her tongue in and out of her mouth.

That's when Lauren said that she thought her big sister had been right and that Evie really **WAS** turning into a fly because she kept buzzing around all over the place and her eyes looked **HUGE**.

At lunchtime, Lauren's big sister Hannah said that we should do a **DOG-POO TEST**. She said that flies **LOVE** dog poo and that if Evie went near dog poo we would know it was because she was turning into a fly.

So Hannah started a game of football and said that one of the goals was going to be **RIGHT** beside the dog-poo bin and the other one was at the other side of the Grassy Bit. Then Hannah said that Evie should be in goal and asked her which goal she wanted to be in. Everyone was

SHOCKED

when Evie chose the dog-poo bin goal! We couldn't **BELIEVE** it. Evie **WAS** turning into a fly!

43

That afternoon we watched a documentary about frogs and their **NATURAL HABITAT** because our topic was

AMPHIBIANS.

We all kept shuffling our bottoms closer to Evie when she wasn't looking. And then we all held our breath, like Sunita had said to do, but we couldn't hear any buzzing noise coming from her.

Then Sunita gasped a bit and whispered something to Jayden King, and told him to pass it on. And when Joel Jack finally passed The Whisper on to me I found out that Sunita thought that Lauren's big sister had got it **COMPLETELY** wrong. And that Evie was actually turning into a **FROG** because

FROGS EAT FLIES!

I looked at Evie. She **DID** look a bit like a frog. Her eyes were **HUGE**. And that's when I remembered that Evie had kept flicking out her tongue when she was watching the cakes baking in the oven and I realised that there must have been a **FLY** nearby and that she'd been trying to catch it.

We know **LOADS** about frogs from doing our topic, so we decided to make a list of what we'd learned about frogs so that we could be a hundred per cent **SURE** Evie was turning into one before we broke the bad news to her.

Jayden King said that frogs had

COLD BLOOD.

So Joel Jack went over to Evie's table and asked to borrow her rubber and when she passed it to him Joel held her hand for a moment before Evie made a face and pulled it away.

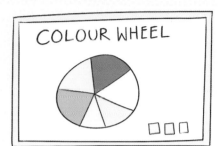

Then Joel ran back over to our table and said, "You're not going to believe this. Evie's hand is **FREEZING!**"

Joel said that it had also been a bit sticky, and that's when Susie Keys started

FREAKING OUT

and shouted,

"FROGS HAVE STICKY HANDS TOO!"

Sunita grabbed Susie and covered her
mouth and said that we didn't want Evie to find
out that she was turning into a frog because
it would be a very big **SHOCK** for her and
that we needed to be **SENSITIVE**.

That afternoon in PE wc were playing basketball with Miss Ranger and Evie was going

WILD.

She was jumping **ALL OVER** the place and Jayden King said that she was jumping so high that he thought he'd seen her touch the net.

By the end of the day, Irfan said that Evie was in the **FINAL STAGE** of turning into a frog because she had a headache and had her head down on the desk.

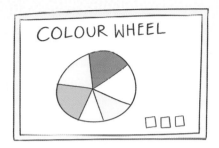

So that's when Miss Riley said that I should take Evie to the nurse. And Sunita said that she should come too in case Evie needed someone to hold her up by each arm. And then Joel Jack and Lauren Carr got to come too so they could hold the doors open. And when we got to the nurse, we told her about Evie turning into a frog because this was getting

SERIOUS.

We said that Evie had swallowed the fly, and told the nurse about how she had been flicking her tongue out trying to catch more flies when we were baking, and about her cold, sticky hands, and jumping high in PE and about her headache and then her being in the final stages of **FROG-TRANSFORMATION**.

HYGIENE

HOW TO GET RID OF NITS

Then Sunita said that the nurse should take Evie's shoes off because she probably had green, webbed feet by now.

The nurse made Evie lie down on the bed for sick people and asked her what she'd eaten today. Evie said that she'd eaten a jam sandwich, a chocolate biscuit, cake mix and jam. Then Sunita reminded her that she'd also eaten a fly.

That's when the Nurse said that sounded like a **LOT** of sugar (apart from the fly) and that it was **NO WONDER** Evie was behaving so strangely. All the sugar had made her

HYPER.

And that's when we realised that Evie had started to act weird after she'd eaten Theo's jam sandwich and Anne-Marie's chocolate biscuit. And that she'd also had

MORE

sugar when she'd eaten all the jam and cake mix when we were baking.

Lauren said that Evie's eyes weren't **BULGING** any more and that they probably only went like that because she was hyper and that she probably **WASN'T** growing frog's legs, and that she was just jumping high in PE because of all the sugar.

Then Joel Jack said, "But why were her hands cold and sticky?"

And Evie said her hands were always cold and that they **WEREN'T** sticky, actually, and that it was **HIS** hands that were sticky. And I thought that Evie was probably right because when I had to hold hands with Joel Jack when we were doing Scottish Country Dancing, I remembered that his hands had been sticky then.

EVERYONE was pleased that Evie wasn't turning into a frog, because everyone **LOVES** Evie as a human girl. So we each gave her a big hug, but then she said she was going to be sick so we let go and the nurse sent us away.

When we got back to the classroom Lauren said, "Did anyone else notice that Evie turned a bit **GREEN** when we hugged her?"

And we all nodded slowly because we **HAD** noticed.

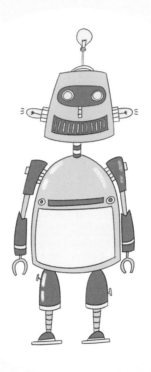

One day Miss Riley was calling our names out because she was taking the register. When she got to Theo Burke, she missed him out, and called Lauren Carr instead.

Sunita Ram put her hand up **RIGHT AWAY** and said, "Miss, you forgot Theo."

And Miss Riley said, "Theo won't be in school today. He's at the hospital."

At first we all gasped (in a bad way) because we thought Theo had maybe broken his leg or all of his ribs or something. But then we all gasped again (in a good way) because we remembered that Theo's mum was **PREGNANT** and that Theo must be at the hospital because his mum had eventually had her

BABY!

EVERYONE started asking Miss Riley what the baby's name was and if it was a boy or a girl. But Miss Riley said that she didn't know and that we'd have to wait and find out the next day.

We all agreed that if it was a boy it should definitely be called Theo Junior and that if it was a girl it should be called Maggie, because that's Miss Riley's first name (even though we're not supposed to know that it is).

Then all of a sudden, Theo appeared at the door with one of the office ladies. Miss Riley wouldn't let him come in right away. She said that she needed to have a **QUICK WORD** with him outside first.

We all knew that Miss Riley probably wanted to be the **FIRST ONE** to know about the baby, and we didn't think that was fair, so we sent Joel Jack up to the door to listen. But Joel said that he couldn't hear anything, and that Miss Riley must be **WHISPERING**.

Then Joel had to run back to his seat as FAST as he could because the door handle started moving.

As soon as Theo walked in we all knew there was something wrong with him because his eyes were too **WIDE** and he was being **WEIRD**.

73

So we asked Theo if his mum had had the baby yet and if his mum was OK. And Theo said that his mum was fine but that she hadn't had the baby yet.

At break time, Theo took his backpack outside with him which everyone thought was weird because none of us **EVER** takes our bag out for break.

Then as **SOON** as we got back into the classroom Theo asked if he could go to the toilet and Miss Riley **LET HIM**. And she didn't say **ANY** of the stuff she usually says if we ask to go to the toilet straight after break, like, "Why didn't you go at break? That's what break is *for*." She just said yes and let him go and we were all **SHOCKED!**

Then when we were working on our project

Theo started **BEEPING!** It was only me and Roz Morgan who heard it, because we were near him when it happened. So we ran over to the Big Table and told everyone who was there, and that's when Joel Jack said, **"LOOK!"** and we looked and saw that Theo was going to the toilet **AGAIN** and that he had his backpack with him **AGAIN**.

That's when Bobby Henderson said that he thought there was something **WRONG** with Theo and that he had **CHANGED**. Bobby said that he didn't know if they were even best friends any more because Theo had been acting **WEIRD** all day and that when he'd sat next to him Theo had **MOVED HIS CHAIR AWAY**.

So as soon as Theo got back from the toilet Sunita Ram and Joel Jack went over to him and said, "Are you still best friends with Bobby?" And Theo said, "Y-e-s," in the **WEIRD** voice.

Then Theo started beeping again and this time we **ALL** heard it!

Theo's eyes went

WIDE

and he looked at Miss Riley and Miss Riley said, "Maybe you should work at the table in the store cupboard, Theo." And Theo got up and rushed into the store cupboard with his backpack on.

Then Joel Jack said, "Miss Riley

KNOWS

there's something wrong with Theo. Why else would she send him into the store cupboard to work on his own?"

That's when Irfan Baxter did a **HUGE** gasp and said, "Theo's been

QUARANTINED!"

But none of us knew what **QUARANTINED** meant, so we didn't gasp.

But then Irfan explained that being quarantined meant that you were kept away from everyone else because you had a

DEADLY
DISEASE

that other people might catch if you touched them or coughed on them. And when Irfan said that we **ALL** gasped.

Susie Keys ran over to her bag and got her **ANTIBACTERIAL HAND GEL** and began rubbing it all over her hands and arms and face.

We all took some too and then me and Bobby Henderson pretended that we needed to sharpen our pencils, even though we didn't, because the bin was right beside the store cupboard. And when we peeked inside we couldn't **BELIEVE** what we saw!

Theo was sitting at the table wearing his backpack … and his backpack was plugged into the **POWER SOCKET!**

That's when Bobby ran over to the others and said, "That's not the **REAL** Theo. That's a

ROBOT!"

That's when we knew that Theo **DIDN'T** have a **DEADLY DISEASE** but was a **ROBOT** instead! That's why he was **BEEPING** and speaking with a weird voice. And his bag was his **BATTERY PACK!**

But then all of a sudden Robot Theo **SCREAMED** and came **RUNNING** out of the store cupboard!

We all watched with our mouths wide open as Robot Theo went

BERSERK!

He jumped up and down and spun round and round and squealed **LOADS**.

That's when Irfan Baxter yelled, **"RUN FOR COVER! IT'S A ROBOT MELTDOWN!"**

So we all hid under the tables and covered our ears because Robot Theo was going to

EXPLODE!

89

But instead of hiding under her desk, Miss Riley ran **TOWARDS** Robot Theo and gave him a great big

HUG!

And that's when Robot Theo shouted, "It's a **BOY!** I've got a **BABY BROTHER!**"

But we were all still a bit worried that Theo might be a **ROBOT IMPOSTER**. So we told Miss Riley about Theo's battery backpack and all the beeping and robot voices. And that's when Miss Riley said that she hadn't wanted to tell us but that it had been Theo's **MOBILE PHONE** we'd heard beeping.

That's when we found out that Miss Riley had **BROKEN THE RULES** because mobile phones are **BANNED** in our school.

Miss Riley said that she really shouldn't have, but that she'd made a **SPECIAL EXCEPTION** and let Theo bring a **MOBILE PHONE** into class as long as he kept it hidden in his backpack. She said that it was so Theo's dad could text him to let him know as **SOON** as his mum had had the baby.

That's when we realised that Theo had been going to the toilet and the store cupboard so that he could check his phone without anyone seeing. And also that he had been speaking weird because he was **NERVOUS** about keeping his phone a secret **AND** about his mum having the baby.

When Theo's dad came to collect him to take him to the hospital he showed Theo a picture of his baby brother. But Theo said that he wanted to show **EVERYONE** his new baby brother so Miss Riley showed us all on the big screen.

But we **GASPED** when we saw the baby!

And then Theo said, "What's his name, Dad?" and his dad said, "Well, we think **ROBERT** is a nice name."

And everyone **BURST** out laughing because **ROBERT** sounds nearly exactly like **ROBOT**!

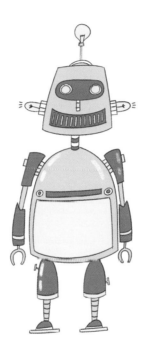

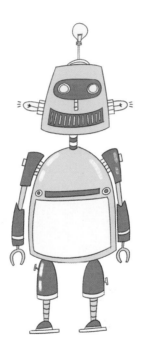

Also by PAMELA BUTCHART and
illustrated by BECKA MOOR

WIGGLESBOTTOM
PRIMARY
THE TOILET
GHOST

PTO for a
SNEAK PEEK!

One time Gavin Ross asked to go to the toilet, and when he came back he was completely **SOAKED**.

That's when Miss Riley said, "What on **EARTH** happened to you, Gavin?"

And Gavin said, "Um. I don't know. I was just washing my hands, and then ...

IT HAPPENED."

So Gavin got sent to the nurse to get changed, and when he came back he was wearing the spare "I-had-an-accident" clothes, and he wouldn't speak to **ANYONE**. We all thought the reason Gavin wouldn't speak to anyone was because the spare trousers were too short.

But then Theo Burke put his hand up and asked if he could go to the toilet and Gavin gasped!

That's when Gavin told us he thought the boys' toilets were **HAUNTED**. Because both taps had come on **FULL BLAST** even though he barely **TOUCHED** them!

But then Miss Riley came over and told us to stop chatting and to go back to our own tables. And then she tried to give the Toilet Pass to Theo Burke, but he said he didn't need to go any more, even though we all knew he did.

At break-time, we all ran outside and sat in the long grass. Sunita Ram said that we should all put our coats around Gavin's shoulders and take good care of him, because of the Toilet Ghost, so we did.